COYOTE STORIES
of the
Navajo People

Edited by   ROBERT A. ROESSEL, JR.
and
DILLON PLATERO

Illustrated by   GEORGE MITCHELL

Published by
Rough Rock Press
(Formerly Navajo Curriculum Center)
RRDS-Box 217
Chinle, Arizona 86503

1991

© 1974 School Board, Inc. Rough Rock Arizona
All rights reserved.
Reproduction in any manner without written
permission of School Board, Inc., is prohibited
except for brief quotations used in connection
with reviews for magazines or newspapers.

Manufactured in the United States of America.
International Standard Book Number: 0-89019-005-4
Library of Congress Catalog Card Number: 68-9678

REVISED EDITION

Printed in the United States of America

Table of Contents

FOREWORD

Coyote Stories IS A BOOK PREPARED PRIMARILY for Navajo boys and girls. However, we firmly believe that it can contribute significantly toward a broader understanding among all people and can be used successfully with non-Navajo students. It is one of a series which presents materials depicting Navajo life and culture.

It is our belief that Navajo youth should have the opportunity to learn about themselves and their culture, as do other American children in other schools.

The Rough Rock Demonstration School, among its many areas of endeavor, is dedicated to the preparation of books and other classroom materials which can be used in schools throughout the Navajo Reservation. By so doing we believe that we can help Navajo children achieve a positive self-image. No person can foretell the future, but everyone knows that tomorrow will be different from today. It is our conviction that we must give to our youth today the tools with which to make intelligent choices. In this way, and in this way only, can Navajo students take their places and be contributing citizens in the world of tomorrow.

We are proud to offer this book as a contribution toward a better future for Navajo youth and toward increased understanding among all people.

TEDDY McCURTAIN, *President*
YAZZIE BEGAY, *Vice President*
JOHN DICK, *Member*
ASHIE TSOSIE, *Member*
BENJAMIN WOODY, *Member*
WHITEHAIR'S SON, *Member*
THOMAS JAMES, *Member*

BOARD OF EDUCATION
ROUGH ROCK DEMONSTRATION SCHOOL

PREFACE

THE BOOK, *Coyote Stories,* IS ONE OF A SERIES being developed by the Navajo Curriculum Center of the Rough Rock Demonstration School, Rough Rock, Arizona. The community at Rough Rock, through the Board of Education, requested a book which would present the traditional stories dealing with Coyote; and the board, responding to the request, authorized this volume.

The members believe that it will add to the understanding and educational development of the children enrolled at Rough Rock, and, furthermore, that it will be very useful in other schools located both on and off the reservation.

One of the principles underlying positive education is the necessity for each individual child to feel a sense of worth, not only in himself and in his family, but in his community and nation. While schools located on Indian reservations usually have units in the lower primary grades dealing with the family and community, I am unaware of any actual published materials which bring together basic history, biographies and other important information dealing with a particular locale and its people.

The purpose of the publications developed by the Navajo Curriculum Center at the Rough Rock Demonstration School is to provide Navajo youth with the same opportunities in education that are provided other American citizens. It is a well known fact that schools and libraries throughout this nation are full of books dealing with the "average American" child. Usually these books illustrate blonde-haired, blue-eyed children running to meet their father when he comes from work. Perhaps these books are effective in promoting the self-image and positive sense of identification for the middle-class blond-haired and blue-eyed individuals reading them. We have no quarrel with their effectiveness for those people, but we have vigorous reservations about these books and their usefulness and appropriateness in Indian education.

It also is a widely known fact that the American Indians, in the past, have been denied an opportunity in school to read and learn about themselves in a positive and meaningful manner. The Rough Rock Demonstration School is aware of this problem, as has been Indian education for decades, and has embarked upon an extensive program of designing, developing and preparing books and other materials dealing with Navajo life, history, biographies, current programs, etc.

The Demonstration School sincerely believes that Indian youth in the past have been denied an equal and proper education because of the inadequacy and inappropriateness of the materials and books used.

Dr. Karl Menninger, perhaps the world's most renowned psychiatrist, long has lamented the fact the Indian education has neglected the fundamental cornerstone on which all education should be based. He believes that Indian education has neglected the Indian child and has made him consciously or unconsciously ashamed of who he is and, therefore, unable to meet the changing world with confidence. Dr. Menninger feels that Indian education should exert every effort to assist the Indian child in being proud of his past and confident of his future.

Without a positive self-image and this affirmative sense of identification, no one, regardless of nationality or background, can achieve his full potential. It is hoped that this book, with other volumes in the series, will trigger throughout the reservations in this nation comparable efforts to prepare materials dealing with the life and culture of our Indian Americans.

ROBERT A. ROESSEL, JR., *Director*
ROUGH ROCK DEMONSTRATION SCHOOL

INTRODUCTION

THIS VOLUME CONTAINS A COLLECTION of fourteen stories which have as their main character "Trotting Coyote." The narratives have been transmitted orally from one generation of Navajos to the next for numberless centuries.

Coyote stories are connected with various ceremonies and are retold when those ceremonies are performed. They also are related, during the winter, by the older generation to the younger generation. The occasion usually is after the evening meal when everyone is settled, the sun has gone down, darkness has fallen and the fire is fully kindled to warm the hogan for the night.

The stories often are narrated when visitors are present, frequently by the visitors themselves. The story-telling guests often are the mother's brothers, the maternal grandmother's brothers and paternal grandfathers. The tales usually are recounted by men but sometimes by women. Because the are told only during the winter (defined as the period between the first frost in the fall and the first thunder in the spring), those who contributed the stories have requested that they be used only during the winter months for instructional purposes.

These tales are part of the enormous mythological treasures of the Navajo people. They are not meaningless folklore or merely colorful cartoons, as the uninformed observer might think. They have great significance to the Navajos because they express, enhance and enforce the morals and norms of Navajo society. They are considered actual occurrences and not the results of artistic imaginations.

"Trotting Coyote" is a representation of socially unacceptable behavior. His ultimate misfortunes are legendary proof of the disastrous effects of antisocial conduct. The ultimate victory and good fortune of those whom "Trotting Coyote" tries to trick, cheat or destroy reaffirms the eventual triumph of justice and morality. The stories thus strengthen and reinforce moral values, social harmony and cultural norms by endowing them with the prestige and power of antiquity, as well as with the sanction and affirmation of the supernatural.

The stories included in this volume have characteristics which are common to the folk tale, the legend and the myth. In their humor, seasonal performance and sociable nature, the coyote stories characterize folk tales. In their somewhat limited sociological and cosmological scope and in their discussion of unusual reality, the stories take on some aspects of the legend. In their association with the ceremonies of the Navajos, and in their explanation and justification of moral values and cultural norms, the stories function as mythology. Mythology serves as a constitution for non-literate societies and embodies the manners, morals, laws and cosmology of a people.

Sincere appreciation is extended to the many persons who contributed to, and assisted with, this volume. The late Albert George, "Chic" Sandoval and John Honie contributed the stories. They were translated by Paul Platero, Della Jumbo and Clark Etsitty. Writing was done by Vada Carlson, Sydney M. Callaway, Andrew Pete, Dr. Grace Langdon and Broderick H. Johnson. Mr. Johnson also supervised the book's publication.

George Mitchell did the very beautiful colored illustrations. Editing was by Robert A. Roessel, Jr.

Dillon Platero, who at present is Deputy Director of the school, was Director of the Navajo Curriculum Center when the stories were collected and written. The local Board of Education and many other Navajos reviewed them.

Everyone who tells these stories does so in a slightly different way, but the real hearts and cores remain relatively unchanged.

GARY WITHERSPOON, *Director*
NAVAJO CURRICULUM CENTER

Rough Rock Demonstration School
April, 1968

Chapter 1

Coyote and the Skunk

One day a Coyote was trotting along in the hot sun. It was near a place called Crystal Mountain (Dzil nilts' ili), which is not far from Cuba, New Mexico. The Coyote was suffering from the heat. He looked up at the sky; there was not a speck of cloud in it.

"I'm being suffocated," the Coyote complained. "I wish a little cloud would appear to shade me as I trot along."

Instantly, a little cloud appeared. However, it was not large enough to do much good.

"I wish a much larger cloud would appear," the Coyote said. "I wish there would be a little breeze to cool me."

The larger cloud appeared, and a breeze cooled the Coyote; but he still was too warm.

"I wish it would cloud up everywhere," he said, "so there'd be no sunshine at all. And I wish a cool breeze would sweep across the whole earth."

When that wish was granted, the Coyote was pleased. He decided to try another wish. This time he wished for a few drops of rain, and these fell immediately. He asked for more, enough to moisten his hair, and this also came to pass.

"Now, I wish a gentle shower would come and wet the earth," the Coyote said, "so that the soles of my feet would be cooled."

Again, his wish was granted.

His feet felt better, but he wanted the wet sand to ooze up between his toes; so this desire was granted also.

His next wish was that the rain would cause water to come up to his ankles, and this happened quickly.

"Now," he said, "let the water rise up to my knees."

The rain came down even harder and soon water was up to his knees as he trotted along.

Then the Coyote decided he wanted even more water.

"I wish it would rain so hard that the water would come up to my belly," he said. And, after that happened, he wished for the water to rise until only his backbone was visible.

By that time it had become a real flood. Water was running very rapidly down all the washes.

The Coyote said, "I wish to float down the stream in the flood waters to a place near some animal homes, like prairie dog towns, or to some other place where there are many small animals I can catch for food."

Then the water rose beneath him and he was carried very swiftly downstream. Suddenly the water swirled him, with some sticks and brush, onto a sandbar and left him there.

He laid there, resting, while the storm passed over, and suddenly he heard a strange noise. He thought it sounded like a ladle (dipper) rattling in a water jug. Looking around, he saw a skunk coming down to the water carrying a jug and a ladle with which to fill the jug.

"Hey, cousin," he called.

The skunk looked all around but did not see the Coyote. Four times the Coyote called before the skunk saw him drying his hair among the sticks and brush on the sandbar.

"Cousin," said the Coyote, "will you get four clubs? Cut some sticks from the brush, then bury them beneath me. There are plenty of small animals around here. We can have a fine feast if you do as I tell you. After you get the clubs, go shake the grasses and get some seeds. Bring them here and sprinkle them around my mouth and nose, and other body openings, to make it seem that I am dead. Then call the animals to come and celebrate my death, and we'll kill a lot of them and roast them."

The skunk went to work and did as the Coyote had told him.

"Now go home and spread the news," said the Coyote. "Tell all your friends and neighbors that the hated one is dead. Tell them you have seen him; then get them to dance around me. When they begin dancing we'll take advantage of them."

4

The skunk hurried home and began telling everyone the Coyote was dead. Some of the rabbits, prairie dogs, rats and mice would not believe it.

"It's a trick," they said. "Coyote can't be killed."

"Come, I'll show you. I have seen him," the skunk said. "He's lying in the arroyo. See for yourselves."

Jackrabbit was the first to investigate. But he was afraid, and he ran past the spot so swiftly that he didn't see Coyote at all.

Cottontail went next, but he saw some weeds to nibble and forgot what he started out to do. He returned, saying that there was no dead Coyote around.

The other animals told the prairie dog to go next. When he got to the edge of the wash he saw the water and wouldn't try to cross it; so he reported there was no dead Coyote around there.

"Well, let's all go together," the skunk said. "I know where he is. We'll put on a big dance around him and rejoice that he is dead."

So they all started out. The skunk led the way. The jackrabbits and the cottontails, the prairie dogs and the rats and the little mice followed.

"Now form four circles around him," the skunk told them, when they had looked at the seemingly dead Coyote. "The little animals will be on the inside, then the next biggest and the next, with the jackrabbits in the outer circle."

The skunk was following the Coyote's instructions. When all the animals began dancing and celebrating excitedly, the skunk was to spray his smell into the air. When it fell, the spray would blind the little animals and he and the Coyote would kill them with the four hidden clubs.

The small animals began dancing with joy around the Coyote, and, when they were all excited, skunk shouted, "Oh, look up into the sky. What a beautiful bird is flying above us."

They all looked up. Then the falling spray dropped into their eyes and blinded them.

While they were crying in pain, Coyote jumped up. He quickly took a hidden club and handed another to the skunk. Between them they soon killed most of the little animals.

When that was finished the Coyote said, "Now, Cousin, you go build a fire over there near the shade, and I'll bring the animals. We'll roast them in a pit."

8

The skunk went out to gather wood for a fire, and soon he had a good blaze going. Then he dug a pit, and he and the Coyote put the animals into it and covered them with the hot coals.

With that finished, Coyote began to figure a way to trick the skunk out of his portion of the meat.

"While we're waiting for the meat to roast, why don't we have a foot race?" he asked.

"Oh, no," the skunk objected. "I can't run fast. I have short legs."

"Yes, that's true," said the Coyote. "So I'll make you a proposition. I'll stay and watch the fire while you get a good head start. We'll run a long race around Crystal Mountain."

The skunk knew the Coyote was trying to trick him. He never could run around that big mountain. But he pretended to believe the Coyote, and meanwhile he was thinking up a good scheme.

"I'll do it," he said, and he started out.

He decided to take his time, go over the nearest ridge, out of sight of the Coyote, and then find a hiding place.

"When Coyote comes along," he told himself, "I'll just let him go by. Then I'll come back, and I'll dig up the meat and eat my share and his too."

When he got on the other side of the ridge he found an abandoned badger hole. Crawling into it, he hid the entrance with a tumbleweed. Then he waited for Coyote.

In a little while along came Coyote. He had tied a cedarbark torch to his tail and was setting everything afire as he ran. The flame touched the tumbleweed over the badger hole and burned it in a flash, but Coyote did not see Skunk peering out at him.

As soon as Coyote ran by, the skunk climbed out and trotted back to the roasting pit. Quickly, he dug up the nicely roasted meat and carried it up among the rocks. Then he took the tails from four of the prairie dogs and buried them in the ashes, so that Coyote would see them and think the meat was still in the pit.

After that, he returned to the rocks and began feasting.

Coyote came dashing back, ran around the fire four times, then laid down in the moist earth in the shade and began rubbing wet sand on his chest. And all the while he was mumbling to himself.

"I wonder where that silly skunk is. I wonder if he really tried to run around the mountain. I wonder if he got lost and never will find his way back."

All this amused him. He was still a little out of breath from his run, and he was overheated because of the torch, but he smelled roasted meat; so he got up and began digging in the ashes.

He pulled out one prairie dog tail and threw it away, saying, "This is no good."

Then, one after the other, he pulled the other three tails out of the ashes. Then he began to suspect something, and he made the ashes fly right and left as he dug for the meat.

When he discovered there was no meat left in the pit, he began looking for skunk tracks. They led him to the rocks. He looked up and saw the skunk sitting there, gorging on roasted meat.

"Cousin," he begged, "Please throw me some meat.

I'm starving and very tired."

At first, the skunk paid no attention to him; but, after Coyote asked four times for meat, the skunk threw him a bone. This happened four times before Coyote finally gave up and went slinking away.

Chapter 2

Coyote and the Cottontail

Coyote was trotting along a little wash one bright sunny afternoon, feeling sorry for himself because he hadn't been able to catch so much as a field mouse or a kangaroo rat all day.

Suddenly, a cottontail jumped from the shade of a clump of sagebrush and dashed away in a great hurry, throwing sand in Coyote's face as he picked up speed.

Coyote was very hungry. Here was a foolish cottontail he surely could outrun. He almost could taste the tender meat he'd soon be having for his dinner.

Sure enough, he soon outran the dodging, terrified rabbit.

"I caught you, Cousin," Coyote said, just ready to sink his teeth into the rabbit. "What a silly rabbit you are. Do you know, I didn't even see you. I'd have gone on past if you hadn't jumped out in front of me."

15

Now he was ready for his feast, but, as he opened his mouth wide to take the first bite, the cottontail began talking. That surprised Coyote so much that he closed his mouth and listened.

"Wait a minute, Cousin," the cottontail said. "As you say, you caught me. So I'm your prisoner. Isn't that true? So, why all the rush to eat me? Let me tell you one thing. You'll be sorry you caught me."

"Why?" Coyote asked.

"Because I'm old and tough. I haven't enough meat on me to make a good meal for a big, strong Coyote like you. But, since you have me, and I can't possibly escape, why don't you stop squeezing my neck so hard and take your claws out of my hide. Then we can talk a little while."

"Talk? What have we to talk about?" Coyote asked, loosening his grip a trifle.

The cottontail was panting, but he didn't want to be eaten. Not if he could help it.

"We can talk about men," he said. "That's it. Men. About the way those creatures live."

"Men? I know more about men than you do," Coyote said, tightening his grip so much that the rabbit kicked and squirmed.

"Well, Cousin, tell me something," the cottontail said. "Loosen up on me a little, and tell me how they carry and use their weapons."

"That's easy. They carry them on their backs," Coyote said.

"That's wrong!" the cottontail said. "You see! I know men better than you do. You don't get close enough to see how they handle their weapons."

Coyote knew this was true. He kept as far away from men as he could. "Now I," chattered the cottontail, wondering how he could keep the Coyote talking until he found a way to escape, "have been very close to men. I have hidden in the brush and watched them pass by me. And I know they carry their bows and arrows in their hands. . . . You're still holding me too tightly, Cousin. Relax a bit, can't you? Just for a few minutes. You know my life is in your hands. There's no need to be so tense. You'll be eating me soon enough.''

Coyote was getting impatient. He wanted his dinner right away. Why should he wait?

However, he said crossly, ''All right, go ahead and tell me how they carry and use their weapons, if you're so smart. But make the story short.''

The cottontail shivered, but he knew he had to be brave if he were to outwit the hungry Coyote.

''I'll tell you, Cousin, They carry the bow in one hand and pull the bowstring and arrow with the other. Then they let the arrow fly. Z-I-N-G!''

Coyote argued with him. He was sure it was not that way.

''The bow and arrow come from over the man's shoulder,'' he said. ''You'd have to prove it to me, if I were to believe it's not that way.''

''Fine! I will,'' the cottontail said. ''For example--do loosen up a little, Cousin--for example, I'd be sitting here, as I am right now, and a man would be watching me. I'd be watching him, too. He would be circling me, getting closer and closer . . . Release me just a bit more, Cousin, while I finish this story . . . Thank you! Now, as I was saying, the man would be circling me. He'd have his bow and arrow in his hand. He'd be all ready to shoot me. I'd be sitting low to the ground, like this. As he slowly brought the bow and arrow up to shoot me, here's what I'd do!''

He jumped out of Coyote's grasp, leaped over that Coyote's shoulder and was off in a flash.

Coyote whirled and ran after him. Time and again he was ready to snap the cottontail up in his jaws, but always the wily rabbit dodged or jumped over a bush.

Finally, the cottontail led Coyote to a place where many small, needle-pointed yucca plants grew. Coyote was close behind him.

The cottontail had to think of something in a hurry. Ahead of him was a small yucca plant, loosened by the wind. He jumped over it and kicked the yucca into Coyote's open mouth.

Coyote thought for a second that he had caught the cottontail. His teeth snapped down on the yucca, and he got a mouthful of sharp yucca needles. Before he could spit them out, the cottontail had run into a crack between two rocks.

Coyote was too large to get into the crack. He could not dig in solid rock. He sat down and began trying to coax the cottontail to come out.

"Hey, Cousin. Let's finish our nice, friendly talk. I don't know when I've enjoyed a talk so much," he said.

"Oh, no! I'm not going out there," the cottontail said. "I'm not that stupid. I know all you want to do is catch me and eat me, even though I am an old bag of bones."

"You look plenty fat to me," Coyote said.

"Well, I'm not. I'm not fat at all. I just look fat because of my thick fur. My fur is much thicker than the fur of other rabbits."

"I'm getting angry with you," Coyote said. "I don't care how thick your fur is. Come out before I smoke you out."

"Oh? Are you going to smoke me out, Cousin," the cottontail teased. "And exactly what do you intend to use for firewood? I don't see a tree closer than a mile away."

Coyote looked around.

Cottontail laughed.

Coyote said, "I will use cedar bark."

Rabbit replied, "That is my food."

"Then I'll use sagebrush," said Coyote.

"That's my food, too," said Cottontail.

"I'll go get some pinon pitch, "Coyote said, "and that surely will do the job."

"So it will," Cottontail wailed, pretending to be terribly frightened. "Unless I get out and run away while you're after the pitch."

"I'll fix that," Coyote said, and he began piling rocks in the crack so that Cottontail was walled into the hole between the rocks. Then he dashed off to the pinon tree in the distance to get some of its sticky pitch.

Coyote, panting, came back with the pitch. Then he used his magic powers to light a fire of twigs and weeds, and he placed the pitch on the fire.

"Oh, I'm as good as dead," the cottontail wailed. "I suppose you intend to blow that thick, black smoke in on me so I can't breathe."

Coyote hadn't thought of that, but it was a good idea. He got close to the fire and began to blow. The smoke came into the crack, where Cottontail got none of it.

21

"Blow harder," the cottontail urged Coyote. "I can't take much more, so you may as well get it over. Come on. Harder. Blow harder. Oh, I'm probably about dead now. This smoke!" He coughed very hard, pretending to be strangling. "Get close to the fire and blow. Blow hard."

Coyote was crouched beside the fire, blowing with all his might. Another minute and he'd have that smart cottontail.

But, when he could hear Coyote blowing as hard as he possibly could, the cottontail gave the rocks a big push, throwing fire and hot rocks into Coyote's face. Then he bounded over his enemy and raced away to safety.

Coyote was busy for some time, cleaning the ashes from his face. He was so angry because he had lost the cottontail that he didn't do a good job of the cleaning. For that reason, even today, Coyote has black streaks down his face.

Chapter 3

Coyote and the Porcupine

When Coyote came trotting through the forest one morning, just at dawn, he saw something that made him very curious. Because he always was curious, as well as hungry, he stopped enjoying the keen fresh air and the smell of sage and cedar, and he trotted over to find what his old friend, Porcupine, was doing.

"Good morning, Porcupine," he said. "I see you have built a nice bark shed for yourself. That is very smart. You like bark to eat. Now all you have to do is tear off a part of your shed and eat it."

"Come in," Porcupine invited. "As you can see, I have nothing to eat in my house, but, since I know you always are hungry, I'll bring you a piece of bark right now."

Coyote thought that was very funny. He did not like bark. Porcupine was teasing him, he decided.

Porcupine waddled outside. He took one of the slabs of bark from his wall, brought it inside and sat down near the fire that was burning in the middle of the shed. Then he pulled a quill from his back and struck the sharp point of it on his nose.

Blood began to come in a red stream which Porcupine caught on the cupped piece of bark. When it was well covered with his blood, he laid the bark gently on a bed of coals and sat back.

"Why did you do that, Cousin?" Coyote asked. "I don't like to see you shed your own blood so carelessly. Are you going to cook your own blood and eat it?"

"Be patient," Porcupine said, leaning back and crossing his legs, "You are about to see something you never have seen before."

Coyote was impatient to find out.

"What?" he said. "What are you going to do? Do you have some magic I know nothing about?"

Porcupine just closed his eyes and seemed to be having a quick nap.

Coyote looked at the bark on the coals. It no longer was bark. It was a delicious roast of ribs, cooking to a nice brown. It smelled good.

Porcupine awoke just as the roast was done. He pulled it from the fire and handed it to Coyote.

"I already had my breakfast," Porcupine said. "So eat all you want, Cousin."

Coyote grabbed the roast and began chewing it. He ate every bit and chewed on the bones.

"That was most delicious, Cousin Porcupine," he said, when he had licked his chops free of every little speck of the roast.

After eating, Coyote said, "Come to my house in four days and I'll see what I can cook for you."

29

On the fourth day Porcupine waddled over to the home of Coyote. To his surprise Coyote had built a bark shed exactly like his own. He even had built a little fire in the shed, just as Porcupine had done.

"Come in, Cousin," Coyote invited him. "As you see, I have nothing in the house for you to eat, but I'll bring in a piece of bark at once."

Porcupine sat down beside the fire and waited.

Coyote rushed outside, humming a song, and soon came back with a large piece of bark.

Then he took a yucca leaf with a sharp point and pricked his nose.

The wise old Porcupine smiled.

"You may be wasting your time, Cousin," he said, as Coyote leaned over the bark with blood spurting from his nose. "Remember, your blood is not the same as mine."

"Blood is blood," Coyote chuckled, placing the bloody bark on the fire. "Now we'll see what kind of a roast I've made."

The bark got hot and the blood began to bubble. Then, suddenly, the bark caught fire and burned brightly. Coyote was horrified.

"What happened? What happened?" he asked, dancing around the fire as the bark turned to ashes. "The bark didn't turn into meat for me. Why not?"

"Not all people have the same gifts," Porcupine answered. Looking very solemn, he got up and waddled away.

Coyote sat beside the fire for a long time. He was terribly unhappy. If the bark would turn to meat for Porcupine, why not for him?

Outside in a pinon tree Bluejay shrieked, ''Squawk! Squawk!,'' and he said, ''You can't have everything, Cousin.''

Coyote didn't want advice just then. He tore a piece of bark from his new shed and threw it at the bluejay.

Then he felt a little better.

Chapter 4

Coyote and the Doe

Coyote was trotting along through the pinon pines and the low growing cedars of his beautiful homeland one morning. He saw a doe, with two pretty spotted fawns, standing in the shadow of a tree.

Coyote looked at the doe, thinking what a lot of meat she would provide for him and his hungry little pups, back in their den with their mother. But there was no use chasing a deer. He could not catch it, unless it was wounded by hunters and could not travel fast, or was very old and ill.

He stopped near the doe and her babies, sat down in the shade and began to talk to her.

"Your children are beautiful," he told her. "They are much more beautiful than my children, though I do admit mine are cunning and cute in their awkward baby way. I suppose your children were just born beautiful."

The doe looked a little nervous. Coyote could not outrun her, but what about her babies? Perhaps he was sitting there, pretending to be friendly, but really planning to catch one of her children.

"No, they were born plain," said the doe. "They weren't just naturally beautiful."

"But how did they get those beautiful spots?" Coyote asked her.

The doe nosed her babies around on the other side of the tree.

"It's a long story," she said, "and I'm sure you wouldn't care to hear all of it. But, in brief, this is the way I did it.

"I found a hole big enough for both of them. Then I gathered cedar wood and bark and built a big fire near them.

"You know, of course, that cedar wood gives off many sparks. Those sparks flew over and landed on my children and colored their skin as you see them."

"But didn't that hurt them? Weren't they burned badly?" Coyote asked.

"Oh, not at all," the doe answered. "Good-bye now, Cousin. I must take my children to the spring for a drink."

She and her twin fawns went bounding away through the forest. Coyote laid down on the grass and looked after them. They were beautiful and they were fast runners. He hoped he could make his children not only beautiful, but less awkward on their feet.

He went home feeling very thoughtful. Maybe he was the only father who thought his babies were ugly. Maybe he'd better take another look at his little ones.

They came tumbling out of the den when he returned home. All of them wanted to be played with, and they tumbled around even more. He looked at them, with his head cocked on one side. They weren't bad. Fat little things. Playful children. Even when he got a little rough in his play they didn't whine or slink back into the den.

However, after the sun had set and the babies were back in the den, sound asleep, he went out and gathered wood for a fire. But he didn't get much that night.

"I'll go get more tomorrow," he told himself.

But the next day he added only a few sticks to the pile of firewood.

It was the same the next day.

On the fourth day he decided he must go through with the plan to make his babies beautiful. He gathered wood and made a big fire around a hole in the sand. Next he carried his children out, each by the back of the neck, and dropped them into the hole.

The babies cried and whined at first, but Coyote could not see them for the smoke.

After a time the fire died down and he went to the edge of the pit to take a look at his babies. He thought they'd be beautiful now, with pretty brown spots on their hides.

What a terrible surprise he got! Instead of pretty spots on their hides, they had no hair at all. It all had been singed off.

"I'll get even with that doe for the trick she played on me," he vowed. But time went on and he never did see her again. Probably she knew how angry he would be and was careful to keep out of his sight.

38

Chapter 5

Coyote and the Lizards

Coyote was always happiest when he was spying on someone or prying into his business. One day, when he saw a group of lizards playing a game that was strange to him, he trotted over to learn all about it.

The lizards were gathered on top of a big, flat rock with one sloping side. They were taking turns sliding down that steep slope on small flat rocks.

Each time, after his slide, the slider picked up his rock at the bottom of the slope and carried it up the hill on his back.

Coyote trotted over to the rock and sat down nearby. The lizards pretended not to see him. They went on with their play, as if he were not there at all.

Coyote didn't like that. He wanted to be noticed at least. He moved a little closer and began talking to the lizards.

"You seem to be having a lot of fun," he said. "What do you call your game."

"'We just call it sliding," one said.

"Sliding, eh?" Coyote was trying hard to be friendly. "It looks so interesting I'd like to join you."

All the lizards turned and looked at him coldly.

"You are not a lizard," one of them said. "Go play your own games. You don't know ours."

"But I can learn," Coyote insisted. "Really, it looks very simple. I'd just stand on the rock and slide down. Let me try it. Just once."

"This game is very dangerous. You'd get killed," and old lizard told him. "The first time you would be all right, but the second time, when you ride the big rock, you'd be smashed flat."

Coyote didn't believe a word of that. None of the lizards had been smashed, so why should he? He kept begging them to let him try it, just once.

"Well, just once, Cousin," said the oldest lizard after hearing Coyote begging. "You can ride the small flat rock, but don't ask to ride the big one."

Of course Coyote intended to ride the big one, also, but he didn't say anything about that at the time. He decided to try the little one, and show them how well he could do it. Then he would persuade them to allow him to try the big one.

The lizards looked sour as they placed the small flat rock in position for him.

"I don't know why you want to play our games," one of them said. "I happen to know you have lots of games to play. I've seen you chasing cottontails and kangaroo rats and all sorts of creatures. I should think running races would be more to your liking. You **are** a fast runner."

Coyote didn't answer. He stepped out on the flat rock. It tilted down onto the runway and--Zi-i-ip!--away he went like a streak of lightning.

Before he reached the bottom of the slide, Coyote jumped off. He picked up the rock and trudged back up the hill with it.

"You see," he panted. "I can do it. Let me use the big rock. Just once."

The lizards looked at him sternly.

The oldest one said, "We warned you. We didn't want you to try the big rock, but your life is your own. If you want to risk it in this way, it is your own fault if you get smashed flat."

The old lizard told the young lizards to get the big rock for Coyote. They moved away silently and came back with it. They placed the big rock on the edge of the runway. Then they stood back.

Coyote was not at all afraid. He ran out onto the rock, tipped it a little, and once more he was sliding very rapidly down the runway. But the big rock caught on a smaller one half way down the slide. The rock flipped into the air, taking Coyote with it.

Coyote was frightened half out of his skin. His ears were flopping and his paws were clawing the air. He wasn't at all proud of himself, as he had been on the first ride.

He hit the ground and rolled over. He saw the big rock coming down on top of him.

"I should have listened," he thought. "I'm going to be smashed flat, just as they said."

Then the big rock fell and smashed Coyote.

The lizards stood looking down at him.

"Poor foolish Coyote," the oldest lizard said. "He's no friend of mine, but still it makes me sad to see him smashed so flat."

"And right in the middle of our runway," said one of the young lizards.

"It wouldn't be right to leave him there. But he's going to be very heavy for us to move," said another.

"It would be simpler to bring him back to life," said a third lizard. "Then he could leave without us having to move him."

"You have a very good idea," said the oldest lizard. "Come on, boys."

Single file they slid down to Coyote and made a tight circle around him so they could work their magic in private. In their own secret manner they brought him back to life.

"Now, go your own way, Coyote," the oldest lizard told him. "And, after this, don't try to play lizard games. We don't want this to happen to you again."

Coyote was glad to be alive. He got up and dashed for home as fast as he could run.

Chapter 6

Coyote and the Beaver People

Coyote was trotting along, sniffing flowers, now and then picking a pretty one to put over his ear.

In the distance, beside a little pool, he saw some Beaver People playing.

He sat on the hillside watching them for a few minutes.

"I do believe they're playing the hoop and pole game," he said aloud, although no one was near to hear him. "I'll just go over and see. It has been a long time since I've seen anyone play that good old Navajo game."

It was true, they were playing that old game.

Coyote trotted over to the beavers in the most friendly way and sat down to watch.

"What are you betting?" he asked. "What does the winner get if he throws the pole through the rolling hoop?"

They looked at him as though they wished he'd go away. One of them finally said, "The winner gets to skin the loser."

"Now that's a little rough, isn't it?" Coyote said. "To lose your hide is bad enough, but to be skinned then and there--well, I don't think I'd like that."

Two of the beavers had rolled the hoop and one of them threw the pole through it. They counted points. Then the winner took the loser aside and began skinning him.

They were at the water's edge as they worked. As soon as the loser was skinned, he rolled into the water, floated around for a little while, gave the water a slap with his broad tail and grew a new skin.

"That's a good trick, if you can do it. Surely, I, with my magic powers, should be able to, and the game looks like such fun," Coyote thought.

The oldest beaver saw the gleam in Coyote's eyes and came over to him.

"If you're thinking of playing the game, do change your mind. Few can do what these players do."

"Oh, come! How about me betting my hide against yours?" Coyote suggested.

"Who would want that rough old pelt of yours?" the beaver asked, looking at Coyote. Coyote's hide certainly didn't look sleek and pretty like those of the beavers. "No, be content to play your own games."

The beaver started to go away, but Coyote ran along beside him, begging to be allowed to play.

After he asked four separate times the old beaver looked at the others.

"Shall we let him play?"

"Yes," one of the younger ones said. "We'll let him win the first time, then we'll win. He won't want to play a third time."

Coyote took one of the poles. He waited until the hoop was rolled, then he dashed after it and threw the pole through it, making many points.

"I told you I could play it," he crowed. "But I'd rather not skin the loser. Let him keep his skin and let me play another game."

"Quit now," said the oldest beaver. "Next time you'll be sure to lose, and I warn you it is very painful for most creatures to be skinned."

"If I lose," Coyote bragged, "I'll jump in the water as you do and grow a new skin."

So they played again. This time a beaver won. He got his knife and walked toward Coyote.

All at once Coyote didn't want to be skinned.

"Now, Cousins, can't you skip this part?" he begged. "I don't like the sight of blood. Particularly when it is my blood. I might even get very ill. YEOW! That hur-r-r-rts!"

Poor Coyote. How he howled and cried and yowled. But the Beaver People had no mercy on him. They just calmly peeled the skin over his head, having a hard time loosening it from his long, slim nose.

When they had finished the job, Coyote jumped into the pool, whimpering, and flopped over on his back as he had seen the Beaver People do. But nothing happened to him. Four times he jumped in and each time he came out as naked as before.

He was terribly worried, and the Beaver People began to feel sorry for him.

"There's only one hope for you," the oldest beaver said. "If we throw you into the badger hole, Badger just may **give** you a new skin. Do you want to try it?"

"Yes," Coyote howled. "Anything. Anything."

So the Beaver People picked him up and carried him to the badger hole and pushed him into it. Then they waited outside. It was a long time before Coyote came crawling out, wearing a new skin. That's why Coyote today has the **same** kind of skin as the badger.

Chapter 7

Coyote and the Wildcat

On one of his many journeys Coyote came upon a wildcat. It was sleeping peacefully on a large flat rock that had been warmed by the sunshine.

Coyote sat down and looked at the sleeping wildcat.

"What can I do to him?" he asked himself. "Ah, I know! I'll push his long nose in; I'll push his long tail in, and I'll pull his short legs out into long ones . . . That will be a joke on him. He won't know what's happened."

Carefully, not making a sound, Coyote crawled across the sand and up to the wildcat. Before the wildcat knew it, Coyote had pushed in its face and tail and pulled its short legs into long ones.

Then Coyote took a sharp stick and pulled some of the wildcat's intestines out, and, using his special magic, he quickly made a fire and cooked the intestines over it.

"Hey, Cousin, wake up! Wake up!" he called to the wildcat. "I've some good food for you to eat."

The wildcat awakened and looked around. He smelled the meat cooking. It smelled good to him.

"This is very kind of you, Cousin," he said, "where did you get the meat?"

"The human beings gave it to me," Coyote lied. "Come on. Eat some. I've already had my fill."

The wildcat ate all of the cooked intestines and licked his lips, saying how good they were.

Coyote rolled on the ground and laughed.

"You were eating your own intestines," he told the wildcat.

The wildcat began to feel sick at his stomach. He tried to spit out the food he had just eaten.

"I didn't swallow them. I didn't swallow them," he told Coyote.

Coyote went away laughing at him, and the wildcat was very angry.

"I'll get even with him!" he declared.

He began following Coyote. Everywhere Coyote went the wildcat followed, slinking through the trees and hiding in the rocks.

Several times he tried to surprise Coyote, and the fourth time his plan worked.

Coyote was asleep after a night of hunting. The wildcat crept up beside him without making a sound. Very gently he stretched the Coyote's nose, then his ears, and, after that, his tail. That's why Coyote's have long noses, ears and tails.

Then the wildcat took a sharp stick and pulled out some of Coyote's intestines, which he roasted over a little fire nearby.

Coyote was as trusting as the wildcat had been. He ate the food offered to him.

Then the wildcat laughed at him, telling him he had eaten his own intestines.

Coyote clutched his stomach, crying, "But I didn't swallow them. I didn't swallow them," just as the wildcat had done.

The wildcat left him there, spitting and mumbling.

Chapter 8

Coyote and the Cornfield

While trotting along through the pinons one day, Coyote saw a wildcat sitting on a high limb.

"Hey, Cousin," Coyote called to him. "What are you doing up there?"

"Looking for food," said the wildcat. "I'm very hungry. I saw this bird's nest up here and thought there might be some little birds in it. But there was nothing but a rotten egg . . . What are you doing, Cousin?"

"I'm on my way to the farmer's cornfield. I'm going to have a dinner of sweet, juicy, just ready-to-eat roasting ears. Why don't you come with me?"

Wildcat came down from the tree and sat near Coyote.

"So corn has ears! Isn't that what you said?"

"Yes. You tear them from the corn stalk, pull the husks back and eat the plump kernels."

"I never thought of eating ears," the wildcat said. "Usually I leave the ears . . . What is corn?"

"The best food you ever tasted," Coyote said, smacking his lips. "And there's so much in one field that you can have all you can hold . . . I hardly can wait. Come on."

"How far is it?" the wildcat asked. "I've had hard luck hunting, and I'm very weak. I doubt if I could run far until I've had something to eat."

It was quite a long way, but Coyote wanted to fool the wildcat.

"Oh, it is only a little way over there," he said, pointing his lips in the direction of the cornfield. "Over a couple of hills."

"But won't the farmer chase you out of the field?" the wildcat asked, still undecided. "As I said, I'm hungry and weak. I won't be able to run very far or very fast."

"The farmer will chase us if he catches us stealing his corn," Coyote said. "I'll help you run fast. I know a magic way."

"Well, all right, then," the wildcat said. "I'll go. But I still don't know what corn is."
Coyote tried to explain.

"First, there's a green cornstalk with nice green leaves. Then a stick grows out of the cornstalk. And on this stick these soft, yellow, milky kernels grow. They're wrapped in husks. You pull the husks back and chew the kernels off the stick."

"Is it all yellow?" the wildcat asked, trotting along beside Coyote.

"No, some of it is white, and--"

"Like snow?" the wildcat interrupted.

"True," said Coyote, "and some of it is red, and--"

"Like blood?" the wildcat asked.

"Yes, and some of it is blue. Like the sky at night."

"I'll go with you all the way," the wildcat said. "I can't imagine that red, white, blue and yellow stuff that's sweet and soft and grows on a stick, but I want to see it and taste it."

With Coyote leading, they ran up one hill, then another and another. The wildcat grew tired. His tongue hung out. He was puffing and panting. He staggered as he ran.

"I can't go any farther, Cousin," he called to Coyote.

"But look!" Coyote encouraged him. "There's the cornfield down below us. That green patch. Surely you can make it that far."

The wildcat was too tired to argue.

"You go on," he said. "I'll come more slowly."

Coyote ran fast down the hill to the cornfield.

"Beautiful! Beautiful!" he said as he reached the first rows of corn. "Yum, yum, yum! I'm glad I'm hungry."

He looked back. He could see Wildcat coming slowly down the hill. Then he began tearing the ears from the cornstalks and eating the juicy corn.

When the wildcat caught up with him Coyote had his mouth so crammed with corn that it dribbled from the corners.

"Help yourself, Cousin," he mumbled and went right on eating.

"I'll rest a little while, first," said the wildcat, flopping down in the shade and going to sleep immediately.

Coyote went on greedily pulling ears of corn from the stalks, stripping back the husks and chewing the kernels from the cobs. He almost had his fill, and his stomach was bulging when he heard the farmer and his three sons coming.

A rock whizzed past his ear. Another went over his shoulder. "Run, Cousin, run," he yelled at the wildcat. "They're after us."

Away he went, sprinting past the wildcat and up the hill, a half-eaten ear of corn in his mouth. The wildcat awoke and began to run for his life.

"What's your magic for running faster?" the wildcat called to Coyote.

The Coyote's mouth was full. He just turned his head from side to side, rapidly.

Wildcat thought he meant that he should, turn his head from side to side in that fashion. He tried it. It made him dizzy. He began staggering. He staggered right off the edge of a little canyon and fell into the branches of a cedar. The farmer and his sons went past him without seeing him.

Coyote was too full of corn. He began to get tired. He knew he had to think of a trick, or the farmer and his three big sons would catch him.

He dropped his ear of corn and began dodging--around this bush, then that rock, then into a gulch and up a hillside. When he thought the farmer and his sons had become confused, he crawled into the deep shade of a bush and lay very quiet.

The farmer and his sons looked and looked, but didn't see Coyote. Soon they gave up and went home.

Coyote watched them disappear over the hill. Then he curled up and went to sleep.

He never did know what became of that hungry wildcat.

Chapter 9

Coyote, Porcupine and the Elk

A fat porcupine was sitting on the bank of the river one morning, wondering how he could get across to the other side. He was hungry. On the other side of the stream were many pinon trees. The porcupine wanted to eat the bark from the trees, but the river was too wide, and the water was high and swift.

Elk were grazing on the flats behind him. Suddenly one elk came toward the river and stopped on the bank near the porcupine.

"Are you going to cross the river?" the porcupine said.

The elk looked down at him.

"Yes, I'm going to cross the river," the elk said.

"Well, Sister," said the porcupine, "will you carry me across? My legs are very short and yours are very long."

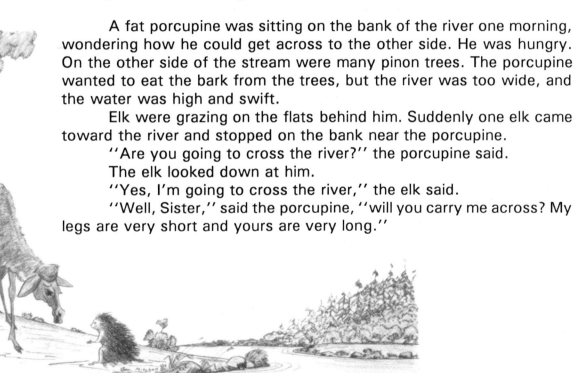

"Yes," said the elk. "You can ride on my back."

"Oh, no," the porcupine cried. "I'd slip off into the water and drown."

"Then you can ride on my horns," the elk told him.

"Oh, no. You'd be sure to shake me off into the water and it would carry me downstream. I'd probably drown," the porcupine objected. "I know a better way. I'll crawl into you from the rear, then I'll crawl out your mouth on the other side."

The elk thought about that.

"No. I don't like that idea," she said. "Your sharp spines might kill me."

"Don't worry about that, Sister," said the porcupine. "Let me show you how easy it will be."

The elk was suspicious at first, then she decided to let the porcupine show how he could do it without hurting her.

The porcupine smoothed his quills down and went in one way and crawled out the other.

"Wasn't that easy?" he asked. "I didn't hurt you at all, did I, Sister?"

"No," she agreed, "but I still don't like the idea. You must be very careful not to extend your sharp spines. But go ahead."

When they got to the middle of the stream the elk became frightened.

"Get out of me," she told the porcupine.

"Stamp your foot," said the porcupine.

The elk stamped her foot.

"I hear water splashing," said the porcupine. "If I came out now, I'd drown!"

The elk went on a little farther, and again said the porcupine must leave her body.

"Stamp your foot," the porcupine told her, as before.

Again he heard water splash, and he refused to leave her.

The elk was close to the river's edge when she again told the porcupine to get out. This time, when the elk stamped her foot, he heard mud splash.

"When you reach dry land, I'll get out," the porcupine promised. But when she stamped her foot on dry land he spread his spines and punctured her insides, and she fell dead. Then he crawled out and began looking for a skinning knife.

Coyote came by as the porcupine was searching for something with which to skin the elk.

"What was that, Cousin?" he asked.

"Oh, I'm just looking for an arrowhead," said the porcupine, not wanting the Coyote to know he had some good meat waiting to be eaten.

"No, Cousin. Didn't I hear you mumbling about a knife? Have you got something to skin? What is it?"

The porcupine saw there was no way to hide the elk from the curious Coyote; so he told the Coyote the truth.

"I killed an elk," he said. "Now I have to find a way to skin it."

"I'll help you, Cousin," said the Coyote.

In a short time they had the elk skinned, and Coyote thought of a way to trick the porcupine out of the meat.

"Let's make a game of this," said Coyote. "Let's play jump-over-the-elk, and the one who jumps over four times without touching the meat gets all of it."

The porcupine didn't want to play that game, but Coyote made it seem so easy that he agreed. He tried and tried until he was exhausted, but he never could jump over the elk's carcass without touching the meat.

Coyote jumped over easily. He cleared the meat four times; then he said, "Well, Cousin, I'm the winner. But I don't want to be greedy. I'll be good and share with you. Here, I'll rip the elk's stomach out and you can wash it in the river; then we'll share."

By that time the porcupine was very hungry. He took the elk's stomach to the river, washed it and then ate it. When he returned to the Coyote he said, "I was washing the elk's stomach in the water when the Water People came up and grabbed it right out of my hands. The Water People swam away, and I suppose they've eaten it by now. But you have meat enough to share, don't you, Cousin?"

The Coyote was very angry. He had intended to eat the stomach himself. He ran down to the river's edge and began cursing the Water People. He used such bad language that they came swimming out to defend themselves.

"We didn't steal your meat," they said. "That porcupine ate it. We saw him."

Then the Coyote became very angry at the porcupine. He ran back, crying out, "So you lied to me! You ate the elk's stomach. The Water People saw you."

"Oh, Cousin," the porcupine said. "You don't think I'd lie to **you**, do you?"

"We'll see whether you lied," Coyote said. "Open your mouth."

When the porcupine opened his mouth, Coyote took a sharp splinter and dug between the porcupine's teeth. Sure enough, he found bits of fresh meat.

"There!" he cried, very angry with the porcupine. "You lied to me."

He picked up a heavy stone and hit the porcupine on the head. When the porcupine seemed dead, Coyote went a little way from the elk and left his waste. Then he started home to get his children and bring them to the elk feast.

Then a voice stopped him. It was saying, "Back to life."

This happened four times and did not stop until Coyote had scattered his waste in all directions. Then he went home.

He got his puppies and brought them to the feast. On the way they kept running off into the grass, catching and eating grasshoppers and other bugs.

"Don't eat those bugs," Coyote scolded them. "They are no good. Come on. I have meat waiting for you."

So they all followed him to the place where he had left the elk and the dead porcupine.

When they reached the river's edge Coyote looked all around and could not see either the porcupine or the elk meat.

Then he looked up, and there was the porcupine, in the top branches of a tree, with all the elk meat beside him. He had been revived by supernatural forces while Coyote was away.

Now it was Coyote's turn to begin begging for meat.

"Cousin, please give me one little piece of meat," he called to the porcupine.

"I'll give you something," porcupine said, and threw down a bone from which he had eaten all the meat.

Coyote chewed it and swallowed it, saying, "This is my chewing bone."

Four times he begged, and each time the porcupine threw down a bone or other waste part of the elk. And still Coyote had nothing with which to feed his hungry children.

70

"Please, Cousin," he begged, "give me a good piece of meat. Can't you see my puppies are very hungry?"

"I'll give you a piece, if you will do one thing for me," answered Porcupine.

"What is that?" Coyote asked.

"That you spread your elk hide under the tree and all of you roll up in it," the porcupine said.

Coyote agreed to that. He dragged his elk hide over to the tree, spread it exactly where he was told to spread it, then he and his puppies rolled up in it.

"Now I'll toss down a really good bone, with meat on it," the porcupine said.

One of the puppies clawed a little peep hole in the elk hide and was looking through it. He saw exactly what the porcupine was about to do. As Porcupine pushed a full quarter of the elk out on the edge of the limb, placing it so that it would fall on the elk hide and its contents, the puppy crawled out and ran away.

The Coyote and all the other puppies were crushed.

"Now," said the porcupine to the puppy who had escaped, "I'll bring you up here and feed you."

He crawled down the tree and carried the puppy up by the back of the neck.

"Eat all you want," he said.

The puppy ate and ate until he was so full he was uncomfortable.

"Take me down to the ground so that I can relieve myself," he said to the porcupine.

"Just crawl out on that branch," the porcupine answered. "That's where you can relieve yourself."

The puppy crawled a little way, but the porcupine kept saying, "Farther! Farther!" until the puppy was on the very end of the branch. Then Porcupine shook it and the puppy fell to the ground and was split open.

The Water People had been watching all this. When the puppy fell, they all shouted, "There goes the clay pot! It's busted!"

Then the porcupine began fussing with the Water People.

"Maybe it's your clay pot that's busted," he said.

The Water People decided to teach Porcupine a lesson; so they sent the beavers to chop down the tree he was sitting in. But each time they chopped down one tree the porcupine went up into another. After they had chopped down four trees, the Water People decided to let the porcupine have his meat in peace.

Chapter 10

Coyote and the Horned Toad

Horned Toad was very busy in her cornfield, where the corn was just ripening. Coyote came to her and said, ''Please give me some of your delicious corn.''

''No,'' said Horned Toad.

Coyote asked her four times; then she picked some corn for him.

''Corn is very hard to raise,'' Horned Toad told him. ''We have to hoe the weeds away from it and pick off the bugs and worms that want to eat it. We even have to water it during dry weather. I can't afford to give all my corn away.''

Coyote kept begging. Horned Toad said he couldn't have any more.

Then Coyote ran out into the field and pulled off a big ear of corn, stripped the husks away and began eating the kernels.

Horned Toad grabbed one end of the ear, and, when he gulped it down, Coyote also gulped Horned Toad down inside him.

Since she wasn't there to scold him, he ate all the corn he could hold. Then he lay down in the shade. He felt very lazy, but when he heard birds flying down to eat the corn, he raised his head and shouted at them.

''Go away! Don't bother my corn,'' he shouted. ''Don't you know it takes work to raise corn? I have to hoe it and water it, and all that.''

Down inside him, Horned Toad made some sort of noise.

Horned Toad was very angry with Coyote and wanted to do something to get even with him. As she lay inside Coyote's stomach, she called, ''Hey, Cousin!''

Coyote jumped up and looked around to see who was calling. He saw nobody, and he lay down again. The second time he heard someone calling, he jumped up again and ran around the edge of the cornfield, looking for the person whose voice he had heard.

This happened four times. The fourth time that Horned Toad called, Coyote realized where the sound was coming from and he looked down at his stomach and asked, "Is that you making noises inside me?"

"Yes," replied Horned Toad. "I'm going to take a little walk down here and see what I can find."

Soon Coyote began to feel strange, and he told Horned Toad to lie down and be still. Instead, Horned Toad continued to walk around, and she tugged at different partes of Coyote's insides.

"What is this?" she asked. "And what is that?"

Each time she gave a little pull at an organ, she hurt Coyote. Once she touched Coyote's heart and asked, "What is this?"

She pulled at the heart, and Coyote shrieked in pain and yelled, "That's my heart."

Horned Toad climbed upward, and when she reached his throat she called, "Now I'm going to cut your throat, Coyote."

"What are you going to cut it with?" Coyote inquired. "I'm not very smart, but I know that you don't have a knife."

Just then Coyote felt something sharp hacking at the inside of his throat, and he began begging Horned Toad not to kill him. The toad was using her sharp horns for cutting.

"Just come out of me," he promised, "and I'll help you raise your corn. I'll hoe the weeds in your garden and water the corn. I'll even bring you some firewood."

Horned Toad replied, "No," and she kept on hacking his throat. Coyote got worried and tried to think of something else that might change the horned toad's mind.

"I'm going to run very fast and make you fall out of my throat," he said. But just as he started to run Horned Toad finished cutting his throat.

When he fell dead, Horned Toad crawled out of Coyote's mouth.

She stood there looking at poor Coyote, lying dead.

"I warned you not to bother my corn," she said. And she went about caring for her cornfield.

Chapter 11

Coyote and the Giant

According to stories of ancient times, cruel giants once roamed the earth. They were especially fond of little children, whom they caught and ate.

One day Coyote was trotting across a rocky place when he saw one of those huge creatures.

"Cousin," Coyote called, "I'm on my way to the creek to take a sweat bath. I admit I was a little afraid to startle such a big, brave giant as you are; so I caught your attention first--will you join me in a sweat bath?"

"Why?" the giant growled, putting his club down and looking more friendly. "Why do I need a sweat bath?"

"Everyone needs a sweat bath," Coyote told him. "They're good for you, Cousin Giant. How else would you be able to get rid of all those no-good things in you?"

"What no-good things?" the giant asked, looking down at his balloon of a stomach.

"You'll find out when you take a sweat bath," Coyote said. "Of course, if you don't want to come with me, I'll trot on by myself."

The giant stopped; then he looked at his big stomach again and thought of all the no-good things that might be in there.

"All right, Cousin," he told Coyote. "Lead the way. I'll follow you."

Coyote trotted off down the hill, being sure to keep a safe distance from the giant's heavy club. When they reached the creek bank, Coyote selected a nice flat place where there were trees and bark and branches. There he could make a sweat house.

"All right, Cousin Giant," Coyote said. "This is an excellent location. You build a fire, while I build the sweat house."

The giant clumsily laid the fire and tried to light it with two flints, while Coyote built the sweat house. After it was completed, Coyote quickly pushed into the house an unskinned leg of a deer that he had hidden.

"I'll trick him!" he chuckled. "He'll never want another sweat bath with me."

Soon everything was ready. Coyote and the giant crawled into the sweat house. It was filled with steam.

"Now what do I do?" the giant asked.

"First," the Coyote told him, "you must drink some of this bitter brew I have prepared for us. It is made of good clean herbs and is wonderful for your system. It will take out all those no-good things I told you about."

"Will it help me catch those fast-running little humans? I like them better than any other food," the giant said. "They almost always run away from me."

"That's because you're so clumsy on your feet," Coyote told him. "Look at me, I can outrun almost anything in the forest or on the desert. That's because I take so many sweat baths."

The giant was big, but not very smart. He believed everything Coyote said.

So they sat in the sweat house, and the steam got hotter and hotter.

"I'm too warm," the giant complained, squirming. "Let's go out and get some fresh air."

"We will," Coyote promised. "But, first, we have to drink more of the herb brew."

The giant shuddered as he drank the brew. He was the first one outside the sweat house.

"Now what do we do?" he asked. "I feel sick at my stomach."

"Wait," Coyote said. "I'll bring dishes, so you can see the no-good things you throw up."

He put dishes before them both. The dishes were curled up pieces of pinon bark. "Now close your eyes, and throw up what is in your stomach."

They both emptied their stomachs, but the giant's waste was clean. Coyote's was filled with worms and other no-good things. Coyote quickly switched dishes while the giant's eyes were closed.

"Oh, Cousin," Coyote cried. "Open your eyes. See what a lot of no-good things you've been carrying around with you. No wonder you're slow on your feet.

The giant looked and heaved some more.

"Maybe we'd better go back in for more cleansing," the giant said.

Coyote was having a hard time to keep from laughing.

"Yes, Cousin," he agreed. "I think we should."

They went back inside the sweat house, where it was pitch dark, and they drank some more brew.

"Now I'll perform one of my miracles," Coyote said.

"Feel my leg . . . that's it! I'm going to break it and then make it as good as ever."

He took a rock and pounded the deer leg until the bone broke. All the time he was pretending to be in great pain.

"Now feel the bone," he said, when he had broken it. "Can you feel it?"

"Oh, yes," said the giant. "You broke it all right."

"Now I'll make it as good as it ever was," Coyote promised. He began spitting on his own leg. "Become whole," he chanted. "Leg, become whole. Be as you were before I began pounding . . . There it is. Now feel it."

The giant reached over in the darkness, and Coyote guided his hand.

The giant felt the leg. He pinched it and pulled it.

"What a miracle," he said at last. "How did you do it?"

"I'll show you," Coyote offered. "Put one of your legs over this way."

Not knowing he was about to be tricked, the giant pushed his leg over close to Coyote.

"It will hurt a little," Coyote warned him. "Especially at first."

The giant's leg was heavy and thick. Coyote pounded and pounded, and the giant yelled and screamed for him to stop.

Soon Coyote felt the bone break.

"There! It is broken. Now start spitting on it."

The giant began spitting. He spat until he ran out of spit, and still his leg was broken and refused to mend.

"Help me, Cousin," he begged. "The magic won't work for me."

"Just keep on spitting," Coyote said, and slipped out of the sweat house.

He knew the poor old giant never would be able to heal his broken leg. Now it would be harder than ever for him to outrun anything--even little human beings.

Chapter 12

Coyote Loses His Eyes

Coyote was walking along one day when he saw some small birds playing a game. They were sliding down a hillside on a rock. As they slid they removed their eyes and tossed them up into the treetops.

Then they said, "My eyes, come back," and the eyes returned to them.

Coyote watched them for a long time. He decided he wanted to play that game.

He trotted over to the players and said, "I want to play that game, too. Please take my eyes out."

"No," they all said, and went on playing.

Coyote kept begging to be allowed to play. The fourth time he asked them they said he could play.

They removed his eyes and handed them to him. As he slid down the hillside he tossed them into a tree. Then he called out, "My eyes, come back to me."

They came back into his hands. Coyote was very excited and wanted to play again.

The small birds warned him, but he wouldn't listen; and the fourth time he slid down the hill the eyes did not come back when he called to them.

"Where are my eyes?" he cried. "Tell me, where are my eyes? I can't go anywhere without eyes."

"We warned you not to play this game," the birds told him, but they felt sorry for him.

"We could make him some eyes," one of them said. "Let's go get some pitch."

They went to the forest and gathered pitch from pine trees, and they pressed it into Coyote's empty eye sockets.

After a while, Coyote could see again. And he disappeared, happy that he could use his new eyes.

Not far away, some people were celebrating and feasting. Coyote, who was hungry, swiftly approached the crowd and asked to help cook the food. They agreed; so he joined the people and assisted with the cooking. In that way he hoped to get something good to eat.

As he went close to the fire, however, his eyes began to melt. He became worried and tried to keep away from the heat. But the people urged him to stay near the fire so that he could help cook.

Coyote faced away from the flames while he tried to turn the meat cooking in the hot coals, and he grabbed a red hot piece of wood, burning his hand. He dropped the coal and yelled.

The people wondered why Coyote was afraid to get near the fire and why he picked up a hot coal. Then they noticed that Coyote's yellow shining eyes were made of yellow pine pitch, and Coyote jumped away from the people and ran off.

That is why Coyote's even today have yellow eyes.

Chapter 13

Coyote and the Woman

Once there was a woman who never had been married. She lived with her four brothers. All day she made baskets. When it was time for the brothers to come from their hunting trips, she set out food she had cooked for them.

One day, while her four brothers were hunting, Coyote came to her house.

"I want to marry you," he told her.

"You'd have to kill the giant, Yeitso, before I'd marry you," she said, feeling certain he couldn't do it.

The Coyote ran off to the place where the Yeitso lived. With his magic tricks he broke off one of the giant's legs. He came back carrying the leg.

"See, I have killed the Yeitso," he lied. "Now I can marry you."

The woman still did not like the idea.

"I'll have to kill you four times, before I can marry you," she said, thinking this would discourage him.

But Coyote knew a magic way to protect his life. He could hide his heart at the end of his tail and each time he was killed he had only to get his heart to start living again.

"Go ahead," he said, "start killing me."

The woman killed him once and he came right back to life. After she had killed him three more times, and he still came back to life, she married him.

That night nothing was cooked for supper for her brothers.

"Why haven't you cooked something for us to eat?" the boys asked her, starting to build a fire.

The woman didn't answer; so Coyote came out of the place where he had been hiding and told them he had married their sister.

"So now I'm your brother-in-law," he told them.

After that they all went out and built a new hogan. Coyote and the woman lived in it.

The next day the brothers went to hunt deer, antelope and mountain sheep. They crept up on the animals, killed and skinned them. Then they wrapped the meat in a sheepskin and made it light with their own secret magic.

"We have some good meat here," they told Coyote. "Take it to your wife, but don't open the package until you get home."

Coyote promised, and then he took the package and hurried over the hill. As soon as he knew the brothers couldn't see him, he broke his promise and opened the package. Then the meat became so heavy he no longer could carry it.

He left it and went to a place nearby, where some spiders were living. He knew they had wanted to marry the sister of the four brothers, and he wanted to brag because he had married her.

"I've married that woman you wanted to marry," he called to them. "Of course, no decent-looking woman would want to marry anyone as ugly as you are."

This made the spiders very angry. They began to hate him and to think up ways to kill him.

"You're a nuisance. Go home," they said.

"We'll talk to him while you make traps for him," some of them told the others, after he had been told four times to go away.

The others hurried out and made four traps with their sticky webs. Then they came back and said, "Now let's kill him with sticks."

They all armed themselves with sticks and ran after Coyote. He got tangled up in the first web, but got out. The second web held until the spiders got close, then he escaped from it, too. He ran through the third trap, also, but he could not kick loose from the fourth one; so the spiders beat him to death with their sticks.

When the brothers came home that evening the sister said, "Where is my husband?"

"I don't know," the oldest brother said. "We killed a mountain sheep and sent the meat home with him."

The sister didn't believe the story.

"Maybe you killed him because you hated him," she said.

Then she turned into a bear and ran out into the forest, looking for him. When she went to the east she grew two sharp fangs, and when she went to the south, she grew two more sharp fangs. After she went to the west she had six sharp teeth, and after she had completed the circle by going to the north of the earth's surface, she had a whole set of eight fangs.

The brothers were afraid of her. The sacred wind had told them she meant to kill all of them; so they put the fourth brother in the fireplace and covered him with earth and ashes, and the rest of them went away, trying to escape. One of them went east, one south and one west. The fourth brother, who was to have gone north, was buried in the fireplace.

The bear, who had been their sister, hunted them down. One by one, she found them and killed them. After she had eaten all of them she returned home and began searching for the fourth brother.

The sacred wind had told him she would look for him and that she wanted to kill him, as she had the others. But the wind also had given him Coyote's secret about hiding the heart, and it had told him where his sister would hide her heart so that she could come back to life, if killed.

When she dug in the fireplace and found the fourth brother, she pretended to be glad to see him.

"Come," she said. "Let me look at your head to see if you have any lice."

The brother knew what she intended to do.

"Let's go outside," he said.

He knelt where he could see her shadow while she looked in his hair. Each time she opened her mouth to bite him, he moved quickly and said, "What's the matter?"

"Nothing," the bear woman said. "I was just looking for lice."

The fourth time she opened her mouth to bite him in the neck, he said, "What are you trying to do?"

"I'm just yawning," she said, but he knew she meant to kill him. Jumping out of her lap, he ran to the place where the sacred voice had told him the woman's heart would be buried.

Quickly he fitted an arrow to his bow and shot the heart, which he could see pulsing and throbbing in its hiding place at the foot of the tree.

The bear woman, not able to restore her life, fell dead.

The young man then cut up her body and threw parts of it to the four directions, scattering the remainder.

"Be useful to human beings as food plants," the brother told the parts.

Some of them turned into pinon trees, full of nuts. Some of them became yucca plants. And all became useful food for human beings for all time.

Chapter 14

Coyote and the Badger

Coyote was trotting along through the country one day, when he met a badger.

"Where are you going, Cousin," Coyote said.

"I have some friends down there in the house you see," said the badger. "I think they will get supper for me. Do you want to come along?"

Coyote always was hungry, so he said he'd go with the badger.

The people were friendly. They cooked food for both of their guests. Badger was bashful. He ate very little. Coyote ate all he could hold.

When they had finished eating, the people said, "Coyote and Badger, go out and hunt some rabbits for us. The one who brings in the most game can marry our daughter."

Coyote liked the looks of the people's daughter. He decided to trick the badger and win the girl. That night he sang for snow, and the next morning everything was white.

Coyote went out very early and began tracking rabbits. He caught one small one, but the others all ran into their burrows and he could not dig deep enough to pull them out.

"I'll dig them out," the badger said. "I have long, strong claws."
He began digging and soon had many rabbits piled up.

"Dig here; oh, dig there!" Coyote kept urging, until badger was getting very weak and tired. Then, once, as the badger went down into a rabbit's burrow, Coyote rolled a big, heavy stone into the hole.

"He won't be able to push that out," Coyote thought, as he picked up all the rabbits and ran off to the home of the people who had the pretty daughter.

"I've brought back many rabbits," he told the people, giving them the animals. "Now I'll marry your daughter."

"Wait until the badger gets back," the people answered, knowing that their daughter preferred the badger to the Coyote. "We'll cook all the rabbits at once when Badger gets back."

Poor Badger. He pushed and pushed backward, but he couldn't push the rock out of the entrance to the hole. Finally, he gave up trying to back out and he began digging in the other direction. He didn't get to the people's house until late at night.

"What kept you so late?" the people asked.

"Coyote put a big rock in the hole I was digging," the badger told them.

"I didn't do that," Coyote shouted, acting very angry. "Badger is making that up."

But the people knew all about Coyote and his tricks. They knew that Coyote had fooled the badger; so they gave Badger the rabbits that Coyote had brought in.

Next, the people told Badger that he could marry the girl because he had the most rabbits.

Coyote was so angry that he tried to keep a fire burning all night so that the others could not go to sleep. And when Badger made him put out the fire, he went on top of the house and looked down at them through the smoke hole.

The next day, when Badger went hunting, Coyote slipped into the house.

"Wouldn't you like to be married to me, instead of to Badger?" he asked the girl Badger had married.

The girl looked at Coyote and turned away.

"No. I wouldn't want **you** for a husband," she told him.

Coyote was surprised. He didn't see why she would like Badger better. But, because she did, he decided he might as well go away.